Medio Pollito

A Spanish Tale

adapted by
Eric A. Kimmel

illustrated by
Valeria Docampo

Marshall Cavendish Children

A hen once laid an egg.

So what? Hens lay eggs all the time.

Not like this! This egg looked like an egg on one side, but on the other, it was perfectly flat. It was as if someone had taken an egg, cut it in half, and covered the open side with a piece of thin paper.

A remarkable egg, all right! However, what hatched out was more remarkable still.

It was a chick who had one leg, one eye, one wing, with half a comb and half a beak. So, of course, they called him Medio Pollito, which means half-chick.

All the other chicks never strayed far from their mother. But Medio Pollito loved to explore. **Hop-step, hop-step, hop-step,** he'd make his way to the road.

"Mother, where does this road go?" he asked the hen.

"I don't know, Medio Pollito," the hen said. "Our friend, the horse, tells me the road goes all the way to the big city of Madrid. That's where the king lives."

"I'd like to see the king," said Medio Pollito. "I'd like to visit the big city."

The other birds in the barnyard overheard him. "Medio Pollito wants to travel to Madrid," quacked the ducks. "He thinks he's a carriage horse and not just a chick."

"He isn't even a chick," honked the goose.

"He's only a half-chick! He won't even get halfway!" gobbled the turkey.

"Don't mind them," clucked Medio Pollito's mother. "You can do anything if you put your mind to it. Why shouldn't you go to Madrid if that's what you want to do?"

"How do I get there?" Medio Pollito asked.

"Follow the road. One step at a time," the hen answered.

So Medio Pollito set out for Madrid. He began following the road, one step at a time, as his mother had told him. **Hop-step, hop-step, hop-step.**

After a while, the half-chick grew thirsty. He stopped to drink from a stream. As he bent down, the stream spoke to him.

"Help me, Medio Pollito," said the stream. "The weeds have choked my bed. I can hardly flow."

"I don't have time to pluck weeds," said Medio Pollito. "I'm on my way to the city of Madrid to meet the king."

"Please!" the stream begged.

"All right, I'll help you," said Medio Pollito. Although he was only a half-chick, he had a whole heart. He plucked and scratched at the weeds until the stream flowed swiftly.

"Thank you," said the stream. "I won't forget you. If you ever need help, call on me."

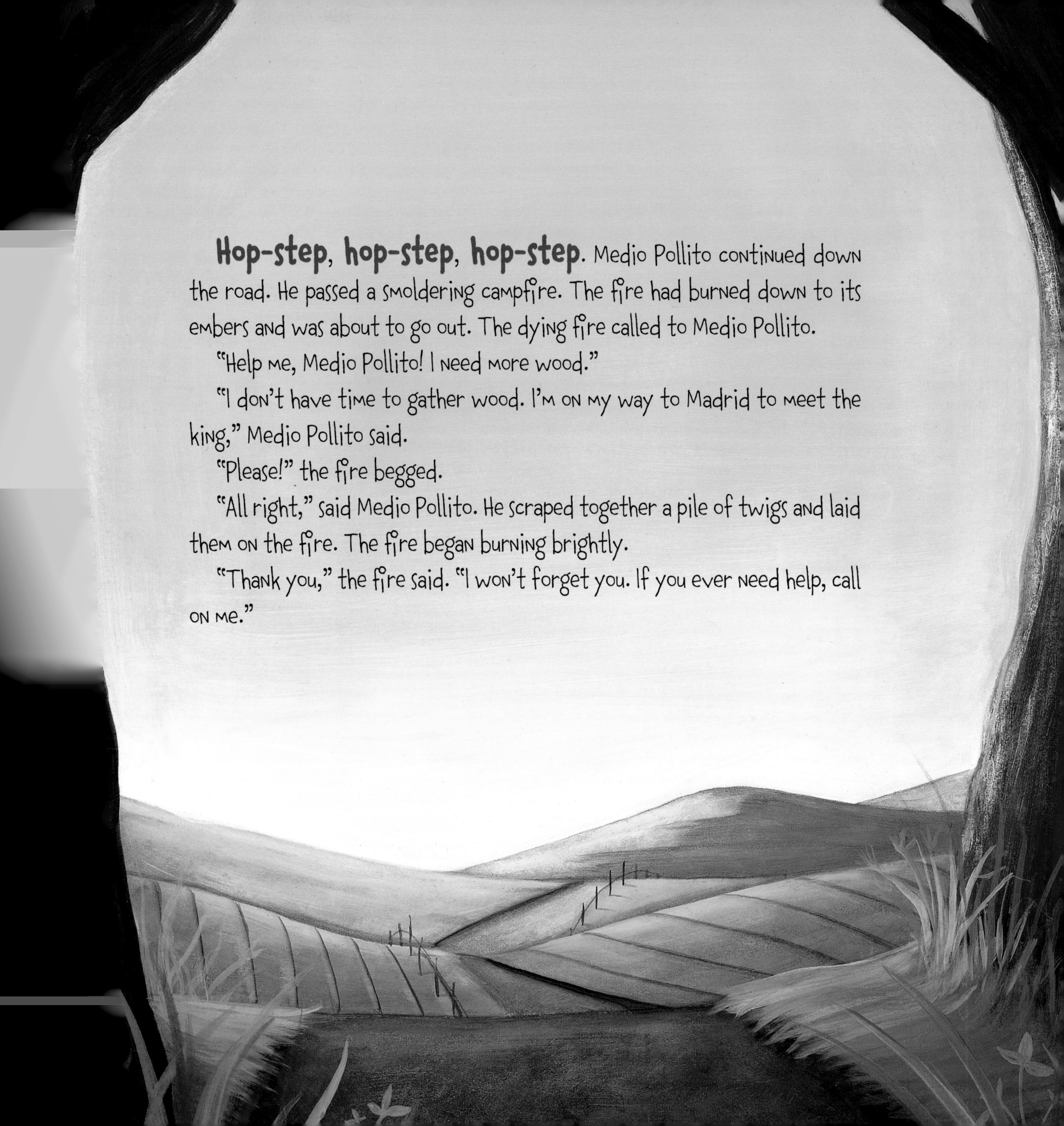

Hop-step, hop-step, hop-step. Medio Pollito continued down the road. He passed a smoldering campfire. The fire had burned down to its embers and was about to go out. The dying fire called to Medio Pollito.

"Help me, Medio Pollito! I need more wood."

"I don't have time to gather wood. I'm on my way to Madrid to meet the king," Medio Pollito said.

"Please!" the fire begged.

"All right," said Medio Pollito. He scraped together a pile of twigs and laid them on the fire. The fire began burning brightly.

"Thank you," the fire said. "I won't forget you. If you ever need help, call on me."

Hop-step, hop-step, hop-step. Medio Pollito continued down the road. He passed a chestnut tree with thick, tangled branches. A voice called to him from the tree. It was the wind.

"Help me, Medio Pollito," the wind cried. "I'm caught in these branches. Can you free me?"

"I don't have time to free you," said Medio Pollito. "I'm on my way to Madrid to meet the king."

"Please!" the wind begged.

"All right," said Medio Pollito. He climbed into the tree and freed the wind.

"Thank you," the wind said. "You've helped me. Now I will help you. I'll take you wherever you want to go."

The wind picked up Medio Pollito and carried him all the way to Madrid.

"Now don't forget," the wind told him when they parted. "Call on me if you ever need a friend."

"I will," said Medio Pollito.

Medio Pollito began exploring the city. **Hop-step, hop-step, hop-step.** He walked through the streets. Soon it was dinnertime. The half-chick felt his half-stomach grumble. "I wish I knew the way to the king's palace. Perhaps the king would invite me to dinner," he said to himself.

As luck would have it, the royal cook came walking by. He overheard Medio Pollito talking. "Would you like to meet the king?" the cook asked.

"That would be wonderful," Medio Pollito answered.

"I'll take you to him." The cook picked up the half-chick and carried him to the palace. But he didn't take Medio Pollito upstairs to the throne room. Instead, the cook brought him downstairs to the kitchen and put him in a pot. He set the pot on the stove.

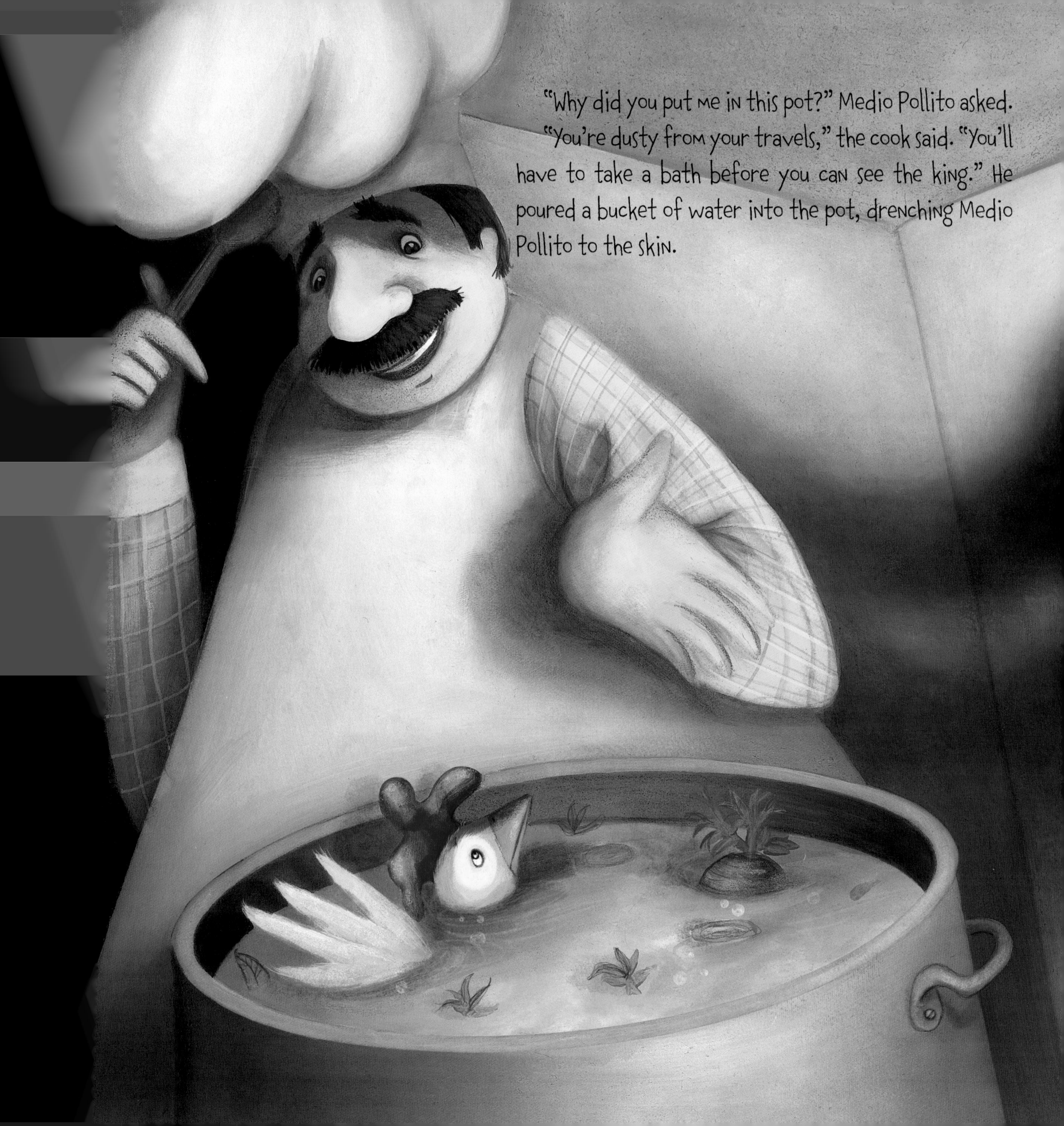

"Why did you put me in this pot?" Medio Pollito asked.

"You're dusty from your travels," the cook said. "You'll have to take a bath before you can see the king." He poured a bucket of water into the pot, drenching Medio Pollito to the skin.

"The water is so cold!" Medio Pollito cried.

"It will soon be warm," the cook replied. He lit a fire in the stove. "The king is not feeling well today," he said. "He asked for a half bowl of chicken soup for dinner. What better way to make a half bowl of soup than with a half-chick? A half-chick is just right for a half-soup!"

The cook slammed the heavy lid down on the pot and left. Medio Pollito was trapped. The water grew warmer. Soon it would begin to boil. That would be the end of him.

"Help me! I don't want to be boiled!" the half-chick cried.

"Medio Pollito! Is that you?"

"Who's that? Who's calling me?" Medio Pollito asked.

"It's me, your friend, Agua, the water!" the water in the pot replied. "Don't be afraid. I will never boil you, no matter how hot the fire gets. Swim around. Enjoy your bath. I promise you will come to no harm."

"Thank you, Agua," said Medio Pollito.

"Who is that? Is that Medio Pollito?" another voice cried.

"Who's calling me?" the half-chick asked.

"It's your friend, Fuego, the fire," the voice answered. "You brought me twigs when I was dying. I will help you. I will sputter and smoke, but I will not flame. No one will cook you, no matter how hard they try."

The cook soon returned. "What is this?" he cried. The kitchen was full of smoke, but the fire did not flame. The water in the pot felt like a warm bath. Medio Pollito, who should have been soup, paddled around like a duck in a pond.

"I've enjoyed my bath," he said. "Will I meet the king now?"

The angry cook plucked Medio Pollito from the pot and threw him out the door. "Find your own way to the king, you miserable half-chick!" he snapped.

Medio Pollito wandered through the streets of Madrid. He felt cold, lost, and very much alone.

"Woe is me!" Medio Pollito sighed. "I don't like the city at all. Why did I leave the barnyard? How will I find my way home?"

"Medio Pollito! Is that you?" a voice asked.

"Who's calling me?" the half-chick answered.

"It's your friend, Viento, the wind. You freed me from the branches. How can I help you?"

"I want to go home," Medio Pollito replied. "I never should have come here."

"Are you giving up so soon? Where is your spirit of adventure?" the wind asked. "Madrid is a wonderful city. Let me show it to you. I'll take you to a place where you can see it all at once."

The wind picked up Medio Pollito and carried him to the tip of the tallest spire on the grandest cathedral in Madrid.

Medio Pollito looked down. He saw the streets, the markets, the plazas, and the palaces stretching far below. "What do you think?" the wind asked.

"It's wonderful!" Medio Pollito exclaimed. "I can stay here forever, perched on this steeple."

"Stay as long as you like," the wind said.

So the half-chick did. There he stands to this day. The wind comes to visit, bringing news of home. The people in the streets and plazas look up to see him talking to the wind. Then they know which way the wind is blowing.

In the whole city of Madrid, there is no finer weather vane than Medio Pollito.

For Shirley, who feeds our sense of adventure
—E.A.K.

For Fanny, who is always there to help others make their dreams come true. "Gracias mamá bataraza!"
—V.D.

A Note about the Tale

The story of "Medio Pollito," the half-chick, is one of the most beloved tales of Spanish folk literature. Traditional versions of this story reflect the rigid, repressive society of Old Spain. Medio Pollito is rude, selfish, and tries to rise above his station. He is drowned, burned, and set on top of the cathedral as a warning to others.

I chose to celebrate the half-chick's spirit of adventure. Why stay in the hen yard when you can have a whole city at your feet?

—E.A.K.

Marshall Cavendish Corporation, 99 White Plains Road, Tarrytown, NY 10591
www.marshallcavendish.us/kids

Library of Congress Cataloging-in-Publication Data

Kimmel, Eric A.
Medio Pollito : a Spanish tale / Eric A. Kimmel ; [illustrated by] Valeria Docampo. —1st ed.
p. cm.
Summary: In this version of the Spanish folktale, Medio Pollito, the half-chick, ventures from his safe barnyard home all the way to Madrid, aided by the friends that he helped along the way.
ISBN 978-0-7614-5705-3
[1. Folklore—Spain.] I. Docampo, Valeria, 1976– ill. II. Title.
PZ8.1.K567Me 2010
2009044621

The illustrations are rendered in acrylic and pencil on paper.
Book design by Anahid Hamparian
Editor: Margery Cuyler

Printed in Malaysia (T)
First edition
1 3 5 6 4 2